Malayan Sun Bears

By Christy Steele

Raintree
A Division of Reed Elsevier, Inc.
Chicago, Illinois
www.raintreelibrary.com

ANIM ... EST

For information, address the publisher:
Raintree, 100 N. LaSalle, Suite 1200, Chicago, IL 60602

Library of Congress Cataloging-in-Publication Data
Steele, Christy.
  Malayan sun bears / Christy Steele.
     v. cm. -- (Animals of the rain forest)
Includes bibliographical references (p.   ).
Contents: Range map for Malayan sun bears -- Malayan sun bears in the rain forest -- What Malayan sun bears eat -- A Malayan sun bear's lifecycle -- The future of Malayan sun bears.
  ISBN 0-7398-6838-1 (lib. bdg. : hardcover)
  1. Sun bear--Juvenile literature. [1. Sun bear. 2. Bears. 3. Endangered species.] I. Title. II. Series.
  QL737.C27 S68 2003
  599.78--dc21
                              2002015212
Printed and bound in the United States of America

Produced by Compass Books

Photo Acknowledgments
Tom Stack/Brian Parker, cover, 1; Wildlife Conservation Society/L. Stark, 6, 29-29; Visuals Unlimited/Barry Slaven, 8; Tom Stack/Mark Newman, 11; Visuals Unlimited/ Mark Newman, 12, 22; Michael Durham, 14, 16, 21; Root Resources/Kenneth W. Fink, 18, 24; Root Resources/Anthony Mercieca, 26.

Content Consultants
David L. Garshelis
Adjunct Associate Professor, Department of Fisheries and Wildlife
Bear Project Leader, Minnesota Department of Natural Resources

Mark Rosenthal
Abra Prentice Wilkin Curator of Large Mammals
Lincoln Park Zoo
Chicago, Illinois

This book supports the National Science Standards.

Some words are shown in bold, like this. You can find out what they mean by looking in the Glossary.

Contents

Range Map
of Malayan Sun Bears

CHINA

VIETNAM

MYANMAR

LAOS

THAILAND

Andaman
Sea

KAMPUCHEA

Range of
Malayan Sun Bears

Surrounding
Land

Water

Borders

BRUNEI

MALAYSIA

MALAYSIA

SINGAPORE

N
W E
S

I N D O N E S I A

A Quick Look at Malayan Sun Bears

What do Malayan sun bears look like?

Malayan sun bears are the smallest kind of bear. They usually have short black hair, but it may be gray or reddish-brown. They have white, yellow, or tan fur around their eyes and noses. Each bear's chest has a white or yellowish-orange marking.

Where do Malayan sun bears live?

Malayan sun bears live in the rain forests of Southeast Asia.

What do Malayan sun bears eat?

Malayan sun bears eat mainly fruit and nuts. They may also eat insects and small animals when fruit is hard to find.

You can see the marking on this sun bear's chest.

Malayan Sun Bears in the Rain Forest

M alayan sun bears are the smallest members of the bear family. They are hard to study in the wild, so we do not know as much about them as we do about other kinds of bears. We know a little from explorers and naturalists that have written about wild sun bears. Still, much of what we know comes from watching sun bears in zoos.

The scientific name for sun bears is *Helarctos malayanus. Helarctos* means having to do with the Sun. They were named this because many sun bears have a marking on their chest that looks like the rising sun. *Malayanus* means Malaysia. Malaysia is where the sun bear was discovered and named by Sir Thomas Stamford Raffles.

Sun bears live in rain forests like this one.
It is easy for them to hide among the trees.

Where do Malayan sun bears live?

Malayan sun bears are found only in
Southeast Asia. They live in many countries,
including Malaysia, Indonesia, Myanmar
(formerly Burma), Cambodia, Laos, Vietnam, and
Thailand. A few sun bears also live in India and
southern China. Sun bears that live on the islands

of Indonesia and Malaysia are often smaller than those that live on the mainland.

Malayan sun bears and spectacled bears are the only bears that live south of the **equator**. The equator is an imaginary line that circles the middle of Earth. It divides our planet into two equal halves called the Northern and Southern Hemispheres. Sun bears live on both sides of the equator in region called the tropics. Sunrise, sunset, and daily temperatures tend to be the same year-round in the tropics.

Malayan sun bears live in tropical rain forests. Weather there is hot and moist. In rain forests, there are two seasons. It is hot and dry during the dry season. It is hot and rainy during the rainy season. Where sun bears live, more than 100 inches (254 centimeters) of rain may fall each year.

What do Malayan sun bears look like?

Most Malayan sun bears are about 2 feet (0.6 meters) tall and around 5 feet (1.5 meters) long. They weigh from 60 to 140 pounds (27 to 63 kilograms), or about the size of a large dog. Because of their small size and short hair, one of their nicknames is "dog bear."

Malayan sun bears have large heads, thick bodies, and short legs. They have large paws with long, curved claws.

Most sun bears have an orange-yellow or white marking on their chest. The shape of this marking is different among individuals. It ranges from a "U" or "V" shape to a full circle. Some circle markings have a dark spot in the middle.

A Malayan sun bear's coat is shiny and thick. Their fur is usually black, but can sometimes be gray or reddish-brown. The fur around their nose and eyes is light yellow, white, or tan. They have the shortest hair of any bear. It only grows to be about .5 inches (1.3 centimeters) long.

A Malayan sun bear's coat helps it survive in its **habitat**. The rain forest is often wet. Short hair dries more quickly than long hair. Also, oil makes the rain and mud flow off the hair

This sun bear's long, curved claws help it hold onto branches.

instead of soaking into the bear's skin. The coat also protects sun bears against insect bites and scratches from branches or thorns.

Dark fur helps **camouflage** the sun bear in the rain forest. Camouflage is coloring or patterns that help an animal blend in with its surroundings. Its fur is dark like the trees and shadows.

▲ **This sun bear is resting in a tree it has climbed.**

Malayan sun bears and trees

Malayan sun bears seem to be more **arboreal** than other kinds of bears. Arboreal means they spend a lot of time in trees. Sun bears climb trees to find food and to escape from their enemies and from biting insects. Trees also provide the bears with cooler, drier places to sleep during the rainy season.

Malayan sun bears have bodies specially suited to climbing. Their long claws dig into the wood and help the bear pull itself up the tree. Their legs are bowed, or slightly curved. Because of their bowed legs, sun bears walk oddly on land. Their toes point inward instead of straight ahead.

Sun bears have very large paws for climbing. The soles of a bear's feet are called foot pads. Thick, furless skin covers a sun bear's foot pads. The tough skin keeps the scratchy wood from hurting the bear. The furless skin may also help the sun bear climb trees. Most other bears have some hair around their foot pads.

Like a bulldog, a sun bear may have wrinkles around its face and neck. This is because it has loose skin that fits like big, baggy clothes. Scientists do not know the use of this baggy skin, but it may make sun bears more flexible. Flexible means something can bend and move around easily.

Sun bears use their long tounges to get food from hard to reach places.

What Malayan Sun Bears Eat

Sun bears are **omnivores**. Omnivores eat both plants and animals.

Sun bears eat nuts, berries, and fruit, such as bananas, coconuts, and papayas. They also eat many kinds of plants, including the growing buds of palm trees. Sometimes when they do this, the palm tree dies. People growing these trees try to keep sun bears away.

Like bears in cartoons, honey is a favorite food for sun bears. Because they like honey so much, "honey bear" is one of their nicknames.

Sun bears may also eat some meat, mainly small animals such as worms, snails, or lizards. They also eat insects such as ants, termites, and beetles. Sometimes sun bears eat carrion. Carrion is the flesh of dead animals.

▲ **Malayan sun bears climb high into trees to find fruit to eat.**

Finding food and eating

Sun bears spend part of their day looking for food. During **mass fruiting**, fruit is easy to find. Mass fruiting happens when most of the fruit trees grow fruit at the same time. At other times, fruit is hard to find. The sun bears then walk around the rain forest to find fruit trees. When they cannot find fruit, they eat other things. Insects are an important food when fruit is hard to find.

A sun bear will climb a tree to eat fruit. It uses its mouth to pick the fruit. Sometimes fruit has a hard covering. Sun bears can smash this fruit with their claws or use their strong jaws to crush the outer shell. They then scoop out the soft inside of the fruit to eat.

A sun bear's teeth are flat for crushing and grinding plants and fruits. This is unlike the sharper teeth of carnivores. These meat-eating animals need sharp teeth to cut and tear meat. Like carnivores, sun bears have four large, sharp "canine" teeth in the front. They use canine teeth for tearing apart logs to find insects. They also break tree branches and fight **predators** with these canine teeth.

The sun bear uses its excellent sense of smell to find insects. Insect nests are often inside trees, under rocks, or inside dead logs. When it finds a nest, the sun bear rips it open with its sharp claws and canines. It then licks up insects with its extra-long tongue. Its tongue reaches up to 10 inches (25 centimeters) and can fit into tiny spaces where insects hide.

Scientists learn about Malayan sun bears by studying bears that live in zoos.

A Malayan Sun Bear's Life Cycle

Scientists have not been able to carefully study the life cycle of wild sun bears. This means that we do not know very much about their mating habits. We also do not know a lot about a cub's life, such as when and where cubs are born. Scientists have learned some things by watching bears in zoos, but this may not be what happens in the wild.

In zoos sun bears may begin mating when they are about three or four years old. In the wild, they are not as well fed. They most likely begin mating at a later age. Mating can happen anytime during the year. Sun bears appear to be the only kind of bear that doesn't have a special mating season.

Young cubs

Mating lasts from one day to a week. During this time, the male and female play with each other. They chase each other, engage in mock fighting, and move their heads up and down.

Females give birth to one or two cubs in a protected den on the ground. A den may be a large hollow log or a space under the roots of a tree.

At about the size of a tomato, newborn cubs are tiny. They weigh about 12 ounces (340 grams). Their skin is pink and hairless, and they cannot open their eyes and see clearly for at least a month. Without their mother, they would not survive. The mother feeds her cubs milk from her body. This is called **nursing**.

When the cubs are old enough to walk, the mother will lead them out of the den. She teaches them how to live in the forest. They start to climb trees when they are still very young.

When the cubs are about two years old, they are fully grown. Then they leave to start a life of their own.

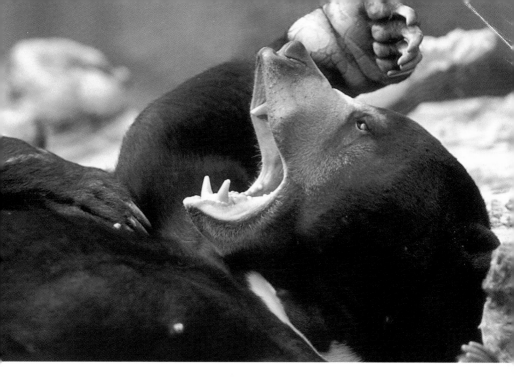

When sun bears are not looking for food, they rest or play.

Sun bears in zoos have lived up to 25 years. Scientists do not know how long wild sun bears live, but it is probably shorter than those in zoos. Wild sun bears may catch diseases that shorten their lives. They also may not be able to find enough food. They will die if they go without food for too long. Some sun bears may also get hurt or killed by **predators**.

Sun bears sleep in trees.

A Malayan sun bear's day

Malayan sun bears may be active day or night, depending on what their environment is like. An environment is an animal's natural surroundings. Like other bears, sun bears are **diurnal**. Diurnal means active during the day. They may switch to being **nocturnal** when people are in the area. Nocturnal means active at night.

Sometimes a tiger may attack a sun bear. When this happens, the sun bear fights to protect itself. It stands up on its two back legs and shows its white chest marking. This makes the bear look larger. It barks loudly at the **predator**. Sometimes this scares the predator away. If the predator attacks, the sun bear will bite and scratch it.

When it is time to rest, sun bears sleep in the tree they are in or find a tree to climb. They sometimes bend and break branches to make a nest. Then, they climb inside the nest to sleep.

Scientists do not know how many sun bears live in the wild.

The Future of Malayan Sun Bears

Once many Malayan sun bears lived in rain forests throughout Asia. Today, scientists do not know how many sun bears are alive in the wild. The sun bear is listed as "data deficient." This means that we know so little about it that we cannot tell whether it is **endangered**. Endangered means an animal may die out. We do know, however, that sun bears face many problems.

Habitat loss is one of the Malayan sun bear's biggest threats. Every year, more Asian rain forest is cut down to build houses and roads. Farmers tear down rain forest plants to create huge farms called plantations. As sun bears lose their habitat, it becomes harder for them to find food. They need food to live and reproduce.

When the rain forest is cut down, sun bears lose places to live.

What will happen to Malayan sun bears?

The future of Malayan sun bears is uncertain. They are at great risk from hunters. Many plantation owners kill sun bears because the bears eat their trees. Other hunters kill sun bears for their body parts. Some Asian people use these body parts to make special medicine. Some people also eat sun bears.

Other hunters try to catch sun bear cubs. Hunters often have to kill the mother bear to get her cubs. This leads to fewer cubs being born in the wild. The sun bear cubs are then sold as pets in Asia. This is a problem because sun bears do not make good pets. Their claws and teeth are dangerous when they grow older. After time, pet owners often sell their sun bears for meat. Some may try to put them back in the wild instead. These sun bears usually cannot survive in the wild because they do not know how to find food.

Some people are trying to save Malayan sun bears. In most countries, there are laws against hunting them. Other countries have special preserves in the rain forest. It is against the law to cut down trees in these places.

In the last several years, some scientists have begun to study Malayan sun bears. Some scientists teach pet sun bears how to live in the wild again. Others put radio collars on wild sun bears to track where they go. They also try to learn what kind of foods the sun bears eat and what **habitats** they need. By doing this, scientists hope to help Malayan sun bears survive in their rain forest habitat for many more years.

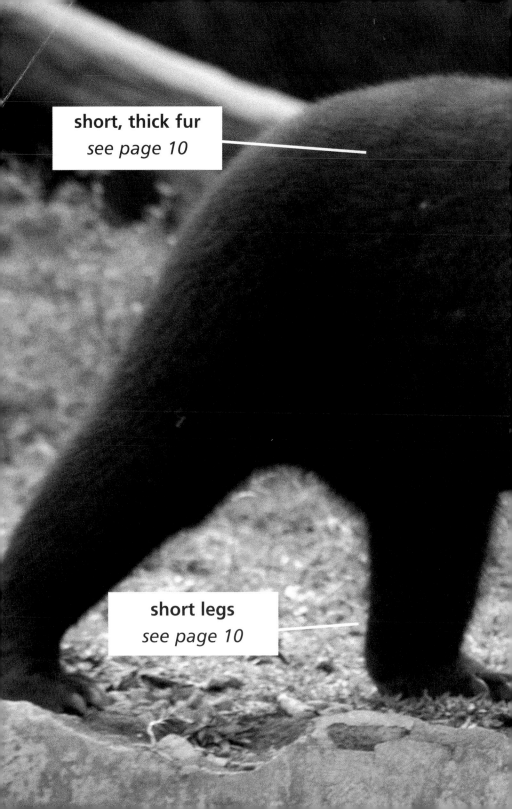

short, thick fur
see page 10

short legs
see page 10

long claws
see page 10

Glossary

arboreal—an animal that spends a lot of time in trees

camouflage—colors, shapes, and patterns that make something blend in with its background

diurnal—active during the day

endangered—an animal that is in danger of dying out

equator—an imaginary line around the middle of earth, halfway between the North and South Poles

habitat—the type of place where an animal or plant usually lives

omnivore—an animal that eats both plants and animals

mass fruiting—a period of time when most of the fruit trees in the rain forest grow fruit at the same time

nocturnal—active at night

nursing—when a mother feeds her young the milk made inside her body

predator—an animal that hunts other animals for food

Internet Sites

Asia Rain Forest—Sun Bear
http://www.oaklandzoo.org/atoz/azsunber.html

Sun Bears
http://www.zoo.org/conserve/sunbear/s_bear.html

Useful Address

Great Bear Foundation
802 East Front
Missoula, MT 59802

Books to Read

Kallen, Stuart. *Sun Bears*. Edina, MN: Abdo & Daughters, 1998.

Legg, Gerald. *Bears*. New York: Franklin Watts, 2002.

Index